For Mum and Dad
and, of course, Sassy, Molly and Milly – P.M.

For Vincent, Oskar and Sputnik – B.T.

First published in Great Britain in 2005 by
Frances Lincoln Children's Books, 4 Torriano Mews,
Torriano Avenue, London NW5 2RZ

www.franceslincoln.com

Distributed in the USA by Publishers Group West

British Library Cataloguing in Publication Data
available on request

ISBN 1-84507-090-9

Printed in China

1 3 5 7 9 8 6 4 2

Flabby Tabby

Penny McKinlay
Illustrated by Britta Teckentrup

FRANCES LINCOLN CHILDREN'S BOOKS

Tabby's life was an endless
round of activity,
from her basket to her bowl,
and from her bowl to her basket...
where she fell asleep.

Sometimes Polly carried Tabby
from her bowl to her basket,
and from her basket to her bowl...

and if she wanted
to get on a chair
Polly was always
there to lift her up...
where she
fell
asleep.

The trouble started the day
Tabby couldn't fit through the cat-flap.
She thought about miaowing,
but decided it was
too much effort.
  'Polly will come along
in a moment,' she thought,
'or my dinner will go down.'

So she
fell
asleep.

Tabby was rudely awoken when
Dad tried to open the door.
He stubbed his toe. Hard.
"Flabby fur ball!" he shouted.
Tabby was offended.

She stalked off to her basket...
and
fell
asleep.

When Tabby woke up she was at the vet's.

"Our cat is too fat," said Dad.

"Would you say she was a very active cat?" asked the vet.

"Well, she's not exactly nimble," said Mum, trying to be kind.

"There is one way to get Tabby fit," said the vet.

Tabby raised an eyebrow... and fell asleep.

It was the most exercise she'd had for a long time.

Some sleeps later Tabby woke
with the feeling that all was not well.
Something furry streaked past
her basket on its way to her bowl.
By the time she got there,
the bowl was bare.

By the time she got back,
the Something was
bouncing in her basket.
It was a kitten.

Before Tabby had time
to protest, the kitten
was off again...

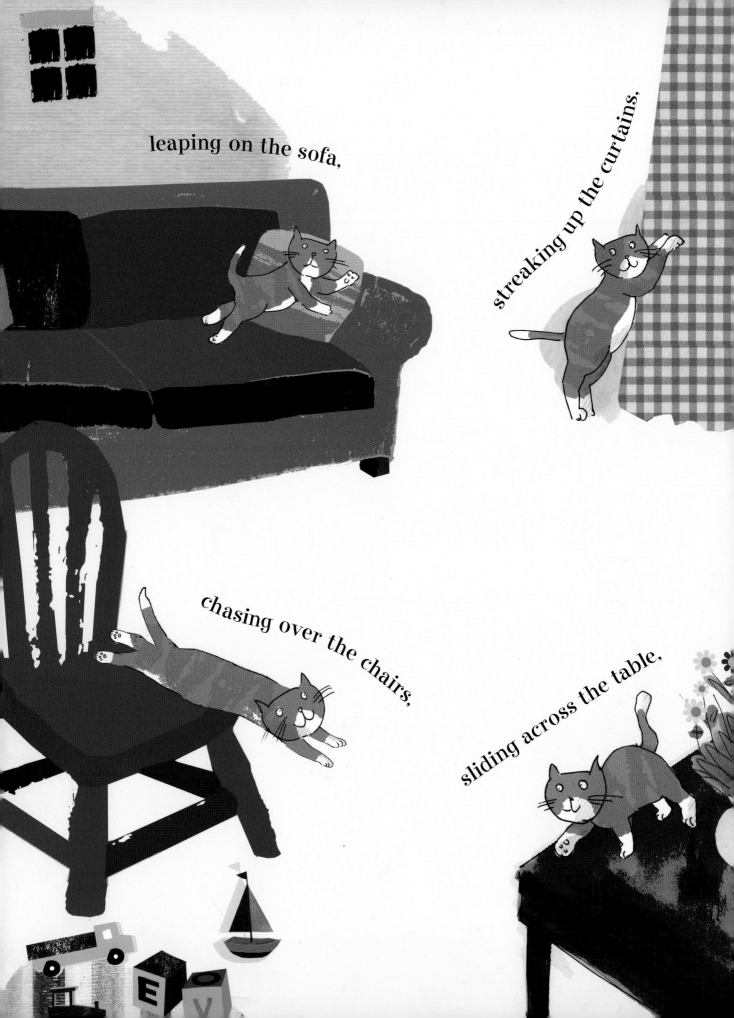

leaping on the sofa,

streaking up the curtains,

chasing over the chairs,

sliding across the table,

balancing along the mantelpiece.

Each time Tabby turned her head to look,
it was gone. She was exhausted just watching it...

She

    fell

        asleep.

Everything changed.

Every time she went to her bowl it was empty.

"I shall starve," Tabby sniffed.

Polly was never there to lift Tabby on to the chair.
She was too busy playing with the kitten.

"I shall waste away," Tabby wailed.

But no one noticed.

Something must be done.
Tabby heaved herself up
on to her paws.
"I'll show them," she sniffed.
So she started Tabby's Secret
Feline Fitness Plan.

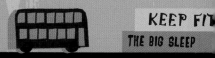

Tabby waddled into the sitting
room and waited behind the sofa.
When Mum came in to do her daily
Keep Fit programme on the television,
Tabby was ready.

On the first day, Tabby struggled
with the stretching.
She fell off the sofa...
and
fell
asleep.

On the second day, she did sit-ups.

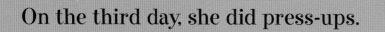

On the third day, she did press-ups.

On the fourth day,
she did star jumps.

On the fifth day,
she managed a gentle jog.

Tabby's Secret Feline Fitness Plan
was working. Tabby was flabby
no longer. Her muscles rippled
under her sleek fur.

"It's time to show Fit Kit what's what," she sniggered.

Next morning, the kitten pranced
past to breakfast. With one bound
Tabby beat him to the bowl.

By the time he got there, the bowl was bare.
"Race you to the basket!" Tabby hissed.
And they were off...

leaping on the sofa,

streaking up the curtains,

chasing over the chairs,

balancing along the mantelpiece,

sliding across the table...

and back to the basket
where, for the first time...

there was room for two.